Yankee Doodle and the Secret Society

by J. J. Bolin

D1369870

Perfection Learning® CA

Cover and Inside Illustration: Rex Schneider

Dedication
To Margaret Anna Bolin, the greatest treasure of my life

About the Author
J. J. Bolin grew up in Marblehead, Massachusetts, a Revolutionary town, and loves stories about the American Revolution. She also writes funny children's poetry.

J. J. Bolin is a lawyer who has investigated and tried fraud cases in court. She started writing poems and stories for children after she read books to her daughter, nephews, and nieces—Megan, Chip, Daniel, Ben, Liz, and Alyse.

J. J. now lives in Iowa with her husband and her daughter. She loves to play the guitar, swim, and play with her two cats, Jasmine and "J. J."

Acknowledgments
I want to thank my OM students, Dana, Megan, Matt, Robert, Kate, Alex, and Glen, for their stimulation and encouragement. Working with such wonderful, creative kids has been one of the great joys of my life. Also, thanks to Jody Cosson, who read my poetry and asked me to write for her. She was a gift to me.

Image Credits: New York Public Library p. 8; National Archives pp. 9, 16; Library of Congress pp. 10, 24, 35, 39, 45, 47, 48, 49, 50, 51, 52, 53, 56

Text © 1997 Perfection Learning® Corporation.
All rights reserved. No part of this book may be used or reproduced in any manner whatsoever without written permission from the publisher. Printed in the United States of America.
For information, contact
Perfection Learning® Corporation,
1000 North Second Avenue, P.O. Box 500,
Logan, Iowa 51546-1099.

Paperback 0-7891-2006-2
Cover Craft® 0-7807-6715-2

11 12 13 14 15 PP 08 07 06 05

Contents

Yankee Doodle

Jauntily

1. Yan-kee Doo-dle went to town A - rid-in' on a po - ny; He
stuck a feath-er in his cap And called it mac-a - ro - ni.

Chorus

Yan - kee Doo-dle, keep it up, Yan - kee Doo-dle dan - dy,

Mind the mu - sic and the step, And with the girls be hand - y.

INTRODUCTION

"Yankee Doodle" is a well-liked children's song. It has been in the United States since the colonial days. But it is much older than that.

The song may have begun during the 1300s in Europe. Two hundred years later, people in Holland were singing it as they worked in the fields.

During the 1600s, the song came to England. New words were written for the tune. They made fun of the English leader Oliver Cromwell. He liked to wear lots of lace and fancy clothes.

In 1755, an English army doctor wrote new words. These words made fun of the untrained American troops during the French and Indian War.

But the American soldiers liked the song! They sang it to their children.

The song was so well liked that it was sung in every camp during the Revolutionary War. The British hated the song. This was especially true when they lost the war!

Children today still love the song. Think about the song as you read about a make-believe Yankee Doodle.

Chapter 1

THE SECRET MEETING

"Come down here, Jeremy! Please.
Get down from the tree!" Yankee Doodle
called quietly.

"Hush! Be quiet. Or go home!"
Jeremy Lowe whispered. "Do you want
them to hear you?"

Boston Common

It was a warm December day in 1773. The tree was on the edge of the Boston Common. The common was a large park in the middle of Boston.

Tall, blond Jeremy was 13 years old. He had already climbed several feet. He was angry with his younger friend, Yankee Doodle. Yankee refused to climb the tree.

Red-haired Yankee Doodle was dressed as fancy as usual. So he decided to wait under the tree.

In the meantime, Jeremy was spying on six men. They were having a meeting below him.

Jeremy could see well from the tree's branches. But he couldn't hear. The men spoke in low voices, all except Samuel Adams. Adams had a loud voice even when he whispered.

Adams was a leader in Boston. He was a tall, strong man dressed in a heavy, brown vest. And his long, brown hair was tied back with a ribbon.

Jeremy listened. But the men were too quiet. And it didn't help that Yankee was being a real pest.

Chapter 2

THE MACARONI

A macaroni

*I*n the 1770s, lots of lace and feathers were common. Both men and women wore them. Sometimes these people were called *macaronis.*

Jeremy was not a macaroni. He never cared about his clothes. His brown coat and hat were plain. His shirt didn't have lace. But worst of all, his hat didn't have feathers.

Yankee liked being called a macaroni. "My new coat and cap feathers are really macaroni," Yankee said to himself. "They are just as nice as those the men in Italy wear."

Yankee thought, "It's the new feathers on my cap. They really make me macaroni!" Yankee felt the feathers and grinned.

Yankee kept asking Jeremy to come down. Finally, Jeremy did.

Yankee groaned. "Jeremy, I don't like being alone down here."

"Then climb with me," Jeremy said.

"I'll get dirty," whined Yankee.

"What! Come on. Don't you want to know about the Sons of Liberty? Don't you want to know what they're up to? Don't you want to be part of the secret society?" asked Jeremy.

"Yes, I do. But I don't want to mess up my clothes," cried Yankee.

"You are a real macaroni!" said Jeremy, frowning. "All you think about are your fancy clothes."

Jeremy put a strong hand on Yankee's back. "Come on," he said. "Let's climb the tree. Hurry."

Yankee stopped thinking about his feathers. "All right," he said. He looked up. Jeremy was on his way up the tree again.

"Jeremy is smart and brave," Yankee thought. "But he is too curious!"

Yankee didn't want to ruin his clothes. Yet he was also a little curious. So he decided to follow his friend up the tree. Maybe they'd find out what the secret society was all about.

A Spy Falls

*Y*ankee climbed to a branch just under Jeremy. They both could see. But they had to strain to hear.

Samuel Adams grinned, "When we're done, the Boston people won't drink tea anymore. Only the Boston fish will drink it!"

Then all the men laughed.

Jeremy and Yankee looked at each other. "What a strange thing to say," they thought.

"Why would fish drink tea?" Yankee thought. "Maybe we're too far away to hear."

George III, King of England

The men were talking about taxes now. They sounded angry. And when they got angry, they also got louder. The boys were glad. Then they could hear what was said.

Yankee looked up at Jeremy. "What are taxes?" he whispered.

Jeremy answered, "Taxes are horrible. They make tea cost more. And I just LOVE tea."

Yankee was mixed up. "But what ARE taxes?" he asked again.

"When you pay for tea, you have to pay some extra money," Jeremy said. "This money goes to King George of England. The money is called a tax."

"What are taxes for?" Yankee was still mixed up.

"King George decides. Some money is used to run the colony. And the king uses some to pay the British soldiers here. But we don't know where all the money goes."

British soldier

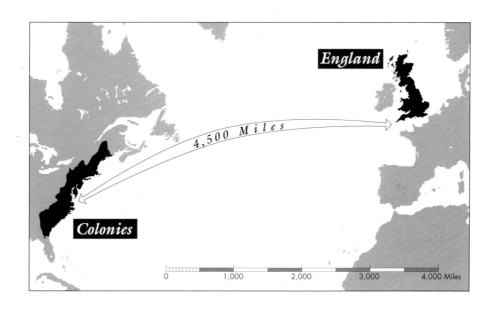

"Oh," said Yankee. He still didn't understand, though. It sounded as if taxes were used for good things. So Yankee asked, "Why are the men so angry about taxes?"

Jeremy shook his head and frowned. Then he answered. "King George lives in England. We live in Boston. And we pay the taxes. But we don't get to decide how the money is spent. And we don't like that."

Just at that moment, Yankee made a big mistake. He reached up to fix the new red feather in his cap. He lost his hold on the branch and fell. Yankee crashed to the grass. He landed right in front of the men!

Chapter 4

UNTIL LATER

*T*hud! All the men turned. Yankee got up quickly and dusted himself off. Then he shivered. His heart was pounding.

Yankee didn't know what the men would do to a spy. And he didn't want to find out. But the men just turned and walked away.

Jeremy came down the tree. He was very angry.

First, Jeremy made sure that Yankee wasn't hurt. Then, Jeremy got really mad. He yelled, "Now we'll never get into the secret society. You really messed this up!"

Yankee hung his head. "I'm sorry, Jeremy." Yankee's head was still spinning from the fall.

"I have to know what it's all about. I'm grown now. And I want to be in the Sons of Liberty," said Jeremy.

Yankee felt very bad. When Jeremy saw his sad face, he said, "It's OK. We'll learn the secret tonight."

Jeremy helped dust the dirt from Yankee's pants and shirt. Yankee felt better. At least he did until he picked up his feathers. One was broken. His sadness returned.

Jeremy patted Yankee on the back. "It's OK, my friend. Let's go home."

Yankee stuck the broken feather in his cap. The boys walked on a path to Tremont Street. "I'm glad Jeremy's my friend," Yankee thought.

As they walked, the boys talked about the secret society. They agreed that they wanted to know more.

Green Dragon Tavern

They knew the Sons of Liberty met at the Green Dragon Tavern. So they planned to meet there later.

"I just have to be a Son of Liberty," Jeremy told Yankee. "I have to know what their secrets are. See you tonight."

Chapter 5

CANDLES, SHADOWS, AND SECRET PLANS

The boys met after dark. They crept behind the tavern to a large oak door. It was pitch black. And the horrible smell from the garbage behind the tavern almost made them sick.

As they stood in the shadows, both boys shook. But it was more from fear than from the cold.

Both boys watched through the crack in the door. Yankee's head was just below Jeremy's. That way they could both hear and see.

Paul Revere

This time Yankee's feathered cap was not in the way. He had left it safe at home.

The back room of the tavern was dark and musty. Several men, including Paul Revere, were there. They stood around a table. The only light came from two candles. Long, dark shadows fell across the floor.

At first, the men whispered. The boys
strained to hear. But soon the men
became angry. They started yelling about
the tax on Boston tea.

Samuel Adams talked the most. He shook
his fist and pounded the table. He raged
about the British, King George, and liberty.

"The British think we will keep paying.
Even if every cent goes to England. We
must stop these taxes!" he demanded.

"We will not pay a cent more after tomorrow night," yelled a short man in a green velvet coat.

Then Thomas Putnam stood up. He spoke to the group. "Let's tell the British we will pay no more! We, the Sons of Liberty, say 'No more.' "

As the men yelled "No more!" together, something strong grabbed Yankee by the neck.

Chapter 6

THE SONS OF LIBERTY

Yankee's shirt choked him. He turned and saw the barman, Gus Thornton. His stringy hair hung in front of his blazing eyes and toothless grin. On his nose, there was a mole with one hair growing out of it.

Gus held both boys by their shirts. They shook with fear.

Yankee took a deep breath and froze. He was sure he'd never breathe again.

Old Gus Thornton dragged the boys through the door. He pushed them toward the table.

Samuel Adams, Paul Revere, and the rest of the Sons of Liberty stopped their meeting. They stared at the boys. Spies! They couldn't believe it!

Adams pointed at Yankee and shouted, "That's the boy from the common. The one who fell from the tree!"

"He was spying then too!" shouted another man.

When the men stopped yelling, Jeremy stopped shaking. He straightened his back and stood up like a man.

Jeremy looked around the room. "All I want to do is help," he said. "I won't tell the British what you're doing. I don't even know what you're doing. But I want to help."

"Why should we trust you?" asked Adams, frowning at the boys.

"Because he wants to fight for freedom!" Yankee said. "And he hates taxes!" A few men smiled.

Joshua Peabody spoke next. "We could let these two take care of the horses and be guards. Paul can't be on the ship and be a guard at the same time."

Boston

ADVERTISEMENT.

THE Members of the Aſſociation of the Sons of Liberty, are requeſted to meet at the City-Hall, at one o'Clock, To-morrow, (being Friday) on Buſineſs of the utmoſt Importance ;—And every other Friend to the Liberties, and Trade of America, are hereby moſt cordially invited, to meet at the ſame Time and Place.   *The Committee of the Aſſociation.*

Thurſday, NEW-YORK, 16th December, 1773.

Notice of a Sons of Liberty meeting
(Note how the letter *s* looks like an *f*.)

That was all Jeremy needed. He stepped forward and said, "I want to be a Son of Liberty."

"Me too," said Yankee. And he stepped up with Jeremy.

"We'll see about that," said Samuel Adams. "We'll see."

Chapter 7

DEEP, DARK SECRET— DEEP, DARK SEA

The Sons of Liberty would not tell the boys what they were planning. But they decided to let the boys help.

Jeremy and Yankee were told to wait near a British ship in the harbor. It had over 300 chests of tea on board.

British soldiers on Boston docks

Jeremy and Yankee went to the docks at sunset the next night. They quietly waited for the men.

They hid behind some large boxes. The boys were excited and a little scared. A British soldier paced back and forth in front of them. But he soon left.

As they waited, it grew colder and darker. The shadows on the wharf made everything look creepy. The water was murky. And a heavy fog moved over the wharf.

Suddenly, a dog ran across the wharf. It scared Yankee, and he almost jumped off the dock. Jeremy grabbed him and pulled him back behind the boxes.

An hour later, a sleepy Yankee put his head on a box. He was almost asleep when he heard a strange sound. He jumped.

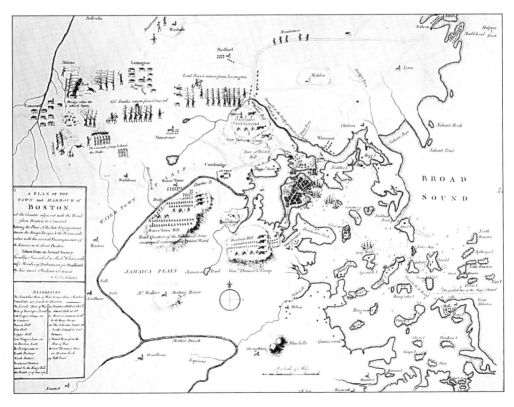

Boston Harbor

Yankee stared into the fog. Suddenly,
he spied several men with hatchets
coming toward him.

Yankee froze. He didn't breathe or move. He just watched the large figures coming. The men had feathers stuck in their hair. Indians!

Yankee gasped. He looked toward Jeremy and whispered, "Help!"

Jeremy, who was just a few feet away, couldn't hear him. Yankee could barely hear himself.

Then he tried again, a little louder this time. He hoped Jeremy would hear.

But then Yankee got a closer look. The men carrying hatchets were not Indians! They were Paul Revere and the Sons of Liberty!

They came over to Yankee. "Have you seen any British soldiers?" Tom Putnam asked.

"One guard," Yankee reported. "But he left."

Putnam told the boys what to do. "You will be our eyes and ears. I want you to hoot like owls if you see anyone. Especially a British soldier."

"And if you do your jobs well,"
Putnam added, "we'll make you Sons of
Liberty." Both boys' hearts beat faster.

Jeremy moved to the other end of the
dock to stand guard. He waved at Yankee.

The men went quietly onto the boat.
They carried the large chests of tea to the
deck. Then they took their hatchets and
cut the chests open. Yankee didn't
understand. Then he remembered—fish
and tea!

The Sons of Liberty dumped the tea
into the sea. They gave it to the fish. No
tea would be sold in Boston for a while.
The fish had it all!

Chapter 8

THE SECRET SOCIETY

When the men were done, they headed for the tavern. There, Paul Revere and the Sons of Liberty made the boys real members of the secret society.

Jeremy stood tall. He felt important. Yankee was proud too.

Later, the boys walked home together in the dark. Yankee wasn't afraid of the noises or shadows. He had grown braver that night. He was thankful that his friend had asked him to go along.

As they walked across the common, Yankee said, "Jeremy, you really need one of my feathers for your hat."

Jeremy patted Yankee on the back and laughed. "No, thank you. There are two boys in Boston who are Sons of Liberty. But there's only one boy in Boston who can be macaroni. And that's you, Yankee Doodle."

Chapter 9

LIFE IN THE COLONIES

Life in Boston in the 1770s was very different from life today.

There were no cars. Some people rode horses. But horses cost money. So most people walked. They walked to work, to school, and to church.

Some people lived in the country. They had to walk to town.

There were no highways. The roads were narrow. They were dusty in the summer and muddy in the spring. They disappeared in the winter!

Everyone worked— men, women, children, and animals.

Some men farmed. Others made wagon wheels and horseshoes. Still others had businesses such as the general store and the barbershop.

People had to make almost everything. Women made soap and jam. They made butter and baked bread. They even made clothes for the whole family. For light, they made candles.

FRONTISPIECE

THE FARMER's WIFE

or

THE COMPLETE

COUNTRY HOUSEWIFE.

CONTAINING

Full and ample DIRECTIONS for the Breeding and Management of TURKIES, FOWLS, GEESE, DUCKS, PIGEONS, &c.

INSTRUCTIONS for fattening HOGS, pickling of PORK, and curing of BACON.

How to make SAUSAGES, HOGS-PUDDINGS, &c.

Full INSTRUCTIONS for making WINES from various Kinds of English Fruits, and from Smyrna Raisins.

The METHOD of making CYDER, PERRY, MEAD, MUM, CHERRY-BRANDY, &c.

DIRECTIONS respecting the DAI-RY, containing the best Way of making BUTTER, and likewise Gloucestershire, Cheshire, Stilton, Sage, and Cream CHEESE.

How to pickle common English FRUITS and VEGETABLES, with other useful Receipts for the Country HOUSE-KEEPER.

Full INSTRUCTIONS how to brew BEER and ALE, of all the various Kinds made in this Kingdom.

Ample DIRECTIONS respecting the Management of BEES, with an Account of the Use of HONEY.

To which is added

The Art of Breeding and Managing SONG BIRDS:

Likewise a Variety of RECEIPTS in COOKERY,

And other Particulars, well worthy the Attention of Women of all Ranks residing in the COUNTRY.

Instructions, full and plain, we give,
To teach the Farmer's Wife,
With Satisfaction, how to live
The happy Country Life.

LONDON,

Printed for ALEX. HOGG, in Pater-noster Row.

(Price One Shilling and Six-pence.)

To tend the Dairy, and the Poultry rear,
Bake, Brew, and hive the Bees in seasons fair,
Taught by our Work, the Housewife learns with ease,
And while she learns still finds her Stock increase.

Book brought from England to help the colonial housewife

47

The children worked too. Those on farms milked cows, gathered eggs, and picked apples and cherries. They helped with housework and other chores. They got wood for the fire. There was no gas heat.

Children worked in town too. They worked in shops. They ran errands.

Some learned a craft such as silver working. These kids were called apprentices. They studied for a long time. When they learned all about the craft, they were called masters.

Many people lived on farms. Farming was hard work. Farmers didn't have tractors. They had to plow the fields with a horse and plant seeds by hand. At harvest time, everyone worked to get all the crops in. Even the children helped.

Schools were very different in the 1770s. They were small with usually only one room. Every grade was in the same room!

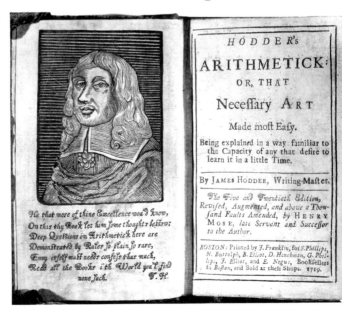

There were only a few books. Everyone shared. Children learned to read, write, and do sums. They read the Bible and other books.

Children didn't go to school very long. There was too much work to be done at home.

Most houses were small. There was a kitchen with a fireplace. In winter, this was often the main room since there was heat.

Women cooked all the meals in the

fireplace. Making a meal took a long time. Everything was made from scratch. There weren't any boxed or frozen foods. And there weren't any fast-food places!

People ate some of the same foods we eat today. They liked bacon and ham.

They ate corn bread. And there was oatmeal for breakfast. Sometimes they had bread with jam.

Most houses had one or two bedrooms. Some houses had a sitting room. Grown-ups sat on chairs. Children sat on benches.

The grown-ups slept in a big bed. The children slept in a small bed that slid under the big bed. It was called a trundle bed.

There was no television or radio. Most children had a few toys. Girls had dolls made from wood. Boys had balls and hoops to roll. There were a few games such as chess. No one had video games!

Children played tag, hide-and-seek, and blind man's bluff. They also ran races.

Many families had pets. They had cats and dogs. Some children had pet rabbits. Some even had pet sheep.

People got sick just like we do. They got colds and flu. But they made cures at home. If children had colds, their mother would rub goose grease on them.

If they had a toothache, they sucked on a clove. Sometimes it didn't help. Then the barber would come. There were no dentists.

Doctor's tools

Barber pulling a tooth

The barber would pull the aching tooth. Many people lost all their teeth at an early age.

Life was hard. But it was an exciting time too. A new country was beginning. The United States was born!

Chapter 10

FREEDOM FROM ENGLAND

There was no United States in the early 1770s. People lived in 13 colonies. And they were ruled by King George of England.

Samuel Adams, Paul Revere, and the other Sons of Liberty were real people. They didn't like being ruled by a king. They wanted to decide the laws.

The Sons of Liberty and many others wanted to be free. Soon, there was a war between the colonies and England. When the Revolutionary War ended, the people in the colonies were free.

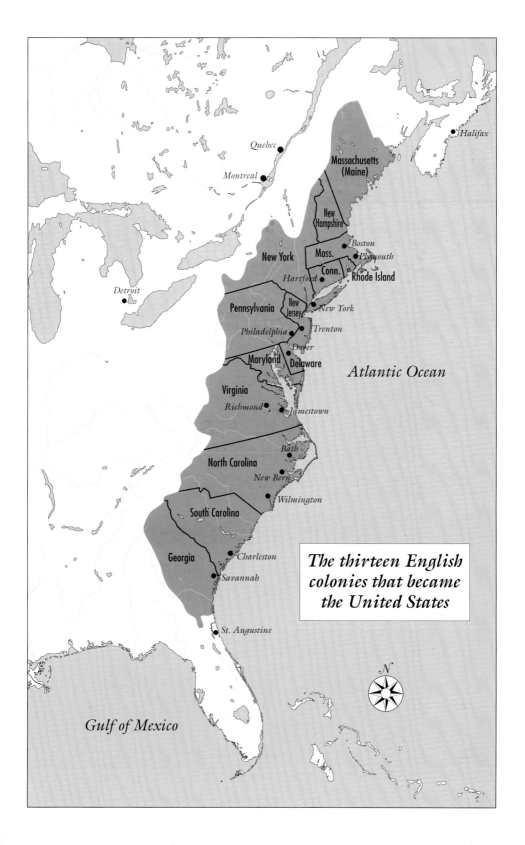

Quebec

Montreal

Halifax

Massachusetts
(Maine)

New
Hampshire

Detroit

New York

Mass.

Boston
Plymouth

Conn.

Hartford

Rhode Island

Pennsylvania

New
Jersey

New York

Philadelphia

Trenton

Dover

Maryland

Delaware

Atlantic Ocean

Virginia

Richmond

Jamestown

Bath

North Carolina

New Bern

Wilmington

South Carolina

Georgia

Charleston

Savannah

**The thirteen English
colonies that became
the United States**

St. Augustine

N

Gulf of Mexico

These colonies became states. And the United States was born. Samuel Adams, Paul Revere, and many others were heroes. We can thank them for the free land we live in today!